Bob 'n John
AT LAKE KITTY PAW PAW

BY MARILYN SADLER • ILLUSTRATED BY ROGER BOLLEN

Troll Associates

Copyright © 1995 by Marilyn Sadler and Roger Bollen.

Published by Troll Associates, Inc. Whistlestop is a trademark of Troll Associates. Bob 'n John is a trademark of Bollen-Sadler, Inc.

Printed in the United States of America.

10 9 8 7 6 5 4 3 2 1

Library of Congress Cataloging-in-Publication Data
Sadler, Marilyn.
Bob 'n John at Lake Kitty Paw Paw / by Marilyn Sadler;
illustrated by Roger Bollen.
p.   cm.
Summary: When their friend Edward the mouse invites them to go fishing, two nap-loving cats spend an adventurous day at Lake Kitty Paw Paw.
ISBN 0-8167-3715-0 (lib.)   ISBN 0-8167-3621-9 (pbk.)
[1. Cats—Fiction.   2. Mice—Fiction.   3. Humorous stories.]
I. Bolen, Roger, ill.   II. Title.
III. Bob 'n John at Lake Kitty Paw Paw.
PZ7.S1239Bo   1995   [E]—dc20   94-33234

Bob and John loved to sleep more than anything else in the world. Every morning, after breakfast, they took a nap under the apple tree behind their house.

Sometimes Bob and John slept until lunchtime. Other times they slept until dinnertime. But usually they slept until one of them was hit on the head with an apple.

One morning, Bob and John had just settled down for nice quiet naps when their friend Edward came along.

"Who wants to go fishing?" he asked.

Bob and John liked to fish. It was something they could do while napping.

So they both said, "We do!"

John made a list of everything they needed
for their fishing trip. He was very organized.

"Sunglasses, lounge chairs, fishing rods . . ."
he said. "Sunglasses . . . I don't see any
sunglasses. . . ."

Everyone wanted to ride in John's pink catillac. It had a very smooth ride. But everyone also knew how fussy John could be.

They did not leave for Lake Kitty Paw Paw until Bob and Edward had been checked for sticky paws.

Soon they were on their way. Everyone was
having a wonderful time. They counted license
plates. They told dog jokes. They even sang "Row,
Row, Row Your Boat."

But when everyone began to sing, John heard more than one squeaky voice coming from the backseat. So he pulled his car off the road and turned around.

To John's surprise, the backseat was filled with Edward's relatives. Even his second cousin on his mother's side was there.

"I'm going to check under the hood," said John. "When I get back, you all had better be gone!"

One by one, Edward's
relatives jumped out of the
car. They were very angry.
They never did like John.

Bob was angry, too.
He did not like to see
John so upset. But at
least he knew that
when John spoke . . .

. . . everybody listened.

Before long they arrived at Lake Kitty Paw Paw. John parked his car and put the top up. He was very tired. Bob and Edward were a little tired, too. So everyone decided to take naps.

But just as they were drifting off to sleep, John's head fell forward against the steering wheel and hit the horn. After that everyone was wide awake.

So Bob, John, and Edward gathered up the lounge chairs and headed down the hill toward the lake.

John took his fishing rod and tossed his line into the air. It sailed out above the water and down into the lake.

Bob took his fishing rod and tossed his line into the air. It sailed out above the water and down into the lake.

Edward took his fishing rod and tossed his line into the air.

It sailed out above the water, crossed over John's line, crossed over Bob's line, and down into the lake.

By the time Bob and John got their fishing lines untangled, it was time for another nap.

Bob and John could have slept until dinnertime. But just as they drifted off to sleep, they were awakened by the sound of barking dogs.

The dogs chased Bob and John around the lake for quite some time.

On their third trip around the lake, John spotted a small rowboat on the shore. He and Bob jumped into the boat and slid out onto the lake.

Bob and John rowed their boat a safe distance from the dogs. Then they settled back and began to fish. But they were very tired from being chased and quickly fell asleep.

The dogs barked for a short time. Then they forgot why they were barking and disappeared into the woods.

Bob and John hadn't been asleep long when, all of a sudden, there was a tug on Bob's line. Bob woke up with a start and lost his balance.

The boat rocked back and forth and up and down until it flipped over, spilling Bob and John into the cool waters of Lake Kitty Paw Paw.

When John woke up, he found himself floating.
"What happened?" he asked.
"I caught a fish!" said Bob.
John wasn't sure whether this was a good thing or not.

Then the fish began to pull Bob in a circle. John had no choice but to be pulled along. Together they spun around and around.

"Let go of your fishing rod!" shouted John. But Bob could not hear him.

Their friend Edward watched everything from the shore. He had not realized how much trouble Bob and John were. But he knew he must help them. There was no telling how long it would be before Bob would let go of his fishing rod.

Edward hurried up a tree. He climbed out on a limb that hung directly over Bob and John. "Grab my paw!" he shouted.

But no matter how hard John tried, he could not reach Edward's paw.

So Edward raced down the tree, up the hill, and over to John's car. All of his relatives were having a picnic in John's backseat.

"Hurry!" he said. "I need your help."

Edward's relatives were very kind. They would do anything for each other.

So they tossed their cheese into the air and hurried after Edward.

Edward and his relatives ran down the hill and climbed up the tree. With Edward leading the way, they stepped out on a limb.

Edward held out his paw to John. Then, one by one, as his relatives stepped closer, the limb bent farther and farther down toward the water until, finally, Edward could reach John's paw!

Then, with the help of his second cousin on his mother's side, Edward lifted John, who lifted Bob, who lifted a nice big fish out of the water.

Soon Bob and John were safe in the tree. John
was so happy to be rescued that he didn't even care
how Edward's relatives got to Lake Kitty Paw Paw
or, for that matter, how the cheese got all over the
backseat of his car.

In fact, he was so happy, he even offered
Edward's relatives a ride home and a big fish
dinner.

Edward's relatives could not have been happier. John wasn't so bad after all.

They jumped into the back of John's car and settled in for the long trip home.

Everyone had a wonderful time. They counted
license plates. They told dog jokes. They even
sang one hundred and one choruses of "Three Blind
Mice." They would have sung one hundred and two,
but John turned on the radio.

Bob and John were very tired. It had been quite a day. But they were happy to know that they would soon be home, in plenty of time . . .

. . . for a nice quiet nap before dinner.